JUMPING IN
A PILE OF LEAVES

DUNDER MAKES
A WISH

Dunder and Munster in

THE RESCUE

Written by Monique Pham-Louie • Illustrated by Byron Louie

MOCHIBOY PRESS

For Dylan, our inspiration

For information regarding special discounts for bulk purchases or to book an event, visit
www.dunandmun.com.

Published by Mochiboy Press, 142 Milpitas Blvd, Suite 134, Milpitas, California 95035
Printed in the U.S.A.

First edition
10 9 8 7 6 5 4 3 2 1

Library of Congress Cataloging-in-Publication Data
Summary: Dunder finds the rescue dog he needs. Munster finds a new family and forever home.
ISBN 978-0-9975118-0-2 (hardcover)
[1. Dogs – Fiction. 2. Pets – Fiction. 3. Animal Rescue – Fiction. 4. Friendship – Fiction.]
I. Title.
2016906593

This is Dunder.

He's an ordinary dog, except for one little thing...

He's a SUPER HERO.

He protects his house from creepy-critters.

Or at least he tries.

Whether he's protecting his toys
from the roaring toy snatcher,

or a deep sea adventure to save Mr. Duck,
Dunder is always in search of a rescue.

Today is a big day for Dunder. His parents are going to the animal shelter to adopt Munster,

a lonely pup who doesn't have a family or a place to call home.

He has been searching for a long time,

but hasn't had any luck. Today, things are about to change.

As Dunder waits at home, he starts to worry about what his new brother might be like.

"What if Munster chews up
all of my toys?"

"What if Munster doesn't like to play super heroes?"

"Or worst of all, what if Munster joins the creepy-critters and chases me?"

HONK! HONK!

Dunder hears his parents pull into the driveway.

He rushes through the hall,
down the stairs, and makes his way
down the porch to see Munster get out of the car.

Suddenly, the creepy-critters see Dunder
and start to chase him again.

When Munster sees this, he starts running and...

WOOF! WOOF! WOOF!

He chases the creepy-critters away.

At this moment, Dunder no longer worried about what his new brother would be like. And Munster knew that he finally found his family, and a place to call home.

Then, the two brothers ran inside,
up the stairs and through the hall to play
super heroes,

while protecting their toys from the roaring toy snatcher.

They even ended the day with a deep sea adventure.

Before going to sleep, Dunder looked at Munster and said, "Good night. Thanks for rescuing me."

Grateful for his home and new family,
Munster replied, "No, thank you for rescuing me."

ABOUT THE AUTHORS

Monique Pham-Louie and Byron Louie live in California's Bay Area with their YouTube® star pups, Dunder and Munster. The family is best known for their time-lapse videos "Puppy to Adult in 40 Seconds" and "Pregnant to Baby in 90 Seconds." They recently welcomed their newborn son, Dylan, into their pack.

"The Rescue" started out as an idea for Dylan's first birthday gift. After receiving several requests from Dunder and Munster's social media followers for a children's book, the family felt compelled to share Munster's rescue story with everyone.

For more Dunder and Munster, visit DunAndMun.com

PARK TIME!

TEAM WORK